Tessa Singh lives in Manchester with her husband, three children and cat. As a teacher of four-year-olds, Tessa sees how books bring so much pleasure and excitement to young children's lives. She wanted to write stories to help children imagine that the world is full of incredible adventures and that they can be the heroes of these stories.

LITTLE BOB SAVES THE WORLD

Tessa Singh

AUSTIN MACAULEY PUBLISHERS™

LONDON • CAMBRIDGE • NEW YORK • SHARJAH

A CIP catalogue record for this title is available from the British Library.

ISBN 9781398431522 (Paperback)
ISBN 9781398431539 (ePub e-book)

www.austinmacauley.com

First Published 2022
Austin Macauley Publishers Ltd®
1 Canada Square
Canary Wharf
London
E14 5AA

For Daynie, Cara and Laura. My wonderful family and friends. Also, for the lovely children I have been lucky enough to teach.

Once in a world full of wonder, there was a little boy called Bob who loved space very much.

One night, Bob kissed Mummy and Daddy goodnight and fetched his rocket which he had carefully hidden behind the bedroom door.

He climbed on board and fastened in his friend Eddie the Elephant who was coming along for the ride. They were on a very important mission to save Planet Earth from a comet that was falling from the skies.

Bob had read all about it in his space book from the library. He had told Eddie the Elephant and together they had made a plan. A very big plan to save Planet Earth.

Bob jumped in his seat ready to launch.
Eddie squeezed his eyes shut.
5, 4, 3, 2, 1... Blast off!

The rocket went shooting past roof tops and trees.
Up, up, up it flew into the night time sky.

Peering through the window, Bob saw twinkling stars and planets of every shape and size as the world shrank beneath him to just the size of a pea.

The universe was so big and Bob had never felt so small.

While Eddie munched on supplies of sandwiches, Bob fetched his telescope and began to look for the comet.

He searched and searched but no matter how hard he tried he could not find it anywhere.

Bob decided to ask for help. He landed on an unknown planet and little aliens came to greet him in a language he did not know. Bob smiled and Eddie gave them chocolate biscuits, which they very much enjoyed.

They listened carefully as Bob told them about their mission to save Planet Earth. The aliens were more than happy to help and pointed Bob in the right direction.

Quick as a flash, Bob thanked the aliens and jumped on board his rocket.

They zoomed through space until they found the comet. Bob could see it racing through the sky like a football on fire.

Bob told Eddie to hold on tight and gave chase as fast as he could.

Finally, the comet was within touching distance. Bob put on his space boots and helmet and went to fetch his giant fishing net.

Bob knew he had to be brave and opened the rocket door. He leant out of the spaceship trying to catch the comet but he missed.

He tried again and again but he was too small to reach. Whatever could he do?

Bob was full of a really big feeling. He thought of all the things he loved about planet Earth. He really wanted to help but he didn't know how.

Just then Bob had a really good idea. He could ask Eddie to help.

Eddie the Elephant wrapped his trunk around Bob's legs and held on tight. Bob stretched as far as he could possibly reach and caught the comet in his net.

Then, with all his might, Bob swung the comet around and sent it flying in the opposite direction.

Bob and Eddie were heroes. The sky lit with a thousand stars and throughout the galaxy little aliens cheered.

Bob squeezed Eddie tight and they celebrated with a chocolate biscuit from the tin. They had saved planet Earth and now it was time to go home to bed.

5/22

CPSIA information can be obtained
at www.ICGtesting.com
Printed in the USA
LVHW070932030522
717813LV00009B/147

9 781398 431522